Samuel French Acting Edition

Amy and the Orphans

by Lindsey Ferrentino

SAMUELFRENCH.COM   SAMUELFRENCH.CO.UK

Copyright © 2019 by Lindsey Ferrentino
All Rights Reserved

AMY AND THE ORPHANS is fully protected under the copyright laws of the United States of America, the British Commonwealth, including Canada, and all other countries of the Copyright Union. All rights, including professional and amateur stage productions, recitation, lecturing, public reading, motion picture, radio broadcasting, television and the rights of translation into foreign languages are strictly reserved.

ISBN 978-0-573-70739-1

www.SamuelFrench.com
www.SamuelFrench.co.uk

FOR PRODUCTION ENQUIRIES

UNITED STATES AND CANADA
Info@SamuelFrench.com
1-866-598-8449

UNITED KINGDOM AND EUROPE
Plays@SamuelFrench.co.uk
020-7255-4302

Each title is subject to availability from Samuel French, depending upon country of performance. Please be aware that *AMY AND THE ORPHANS* may not be licensed by Samuel French in your territory. Professional and amateur producers should contact the nearest Samuel French office or licensing partner to verify availability.

CAUTION: Professional and amateur producers are hereby warned that *AMY AND THE ORPHANS* is subject to a licensing fee. Publication of this play(s) does not imply availability for performance. Both amateurs and professionals considering a production are strongly advised to apply to Samuel French before starting rehearsals, advertising, or booking a theatre. A licensing fee must be paid whether the title(s) is presented for charity or gain and whether or not admission is charged. Professional/ Stock licensing fees are quoted upon application to Samuel French.

No one shall make any changes in this title(s) for the purpose of production. No part of this book may be reproduced, stored in a retrieval system, or transmitted in any form, by any means, now known or yet to be invented, including mechanical, electronic, photocopying, recording, videotaping, or otherwise, without the prior written permission of the publisher. No one shall upload this title(s), or part of this title(s), to any social media websites.

For all enquiries regarding motion picture, television, and other media rights, please contact Samuel French.

MUSIC USE NOTE

Licensees are solely responsible for obtaining formal written permission from copyright owners to use copyrighted music in the performance of this play and are strongly cautioned to do so. If no such permission is obtained by the licensee, then the licensee must use only original music that the licensee owns and controls. Licensees are solely responsible and liable for all music clearances and shall indemnify the copyright owners of the play(s) and their licensing agent, Samuel French, against any costs, expenses, losses and liabilities arising from the use of music by licensees. Please contact the appropriate music licensing authority in your territory for the rights to any incidental music.

IMPORTANT BILLING AND CREDIT REQUIREMENTS

If you have obtained performance rights to this title, please refer to your licensing agreement for important billing and credit requirements.

AMY AND THE ORPHANS was commissioned and originally produced by Roundabout Theatre Company (Todd Haimes, Artistic Director; Harold Wolpert, Managing Director; Julia C. Levy, Executive Director; Sydney Beers, General Manager) at the Laura Pels Theatre on March 1, 2018. The production was directed by Scott Ellis, with sets by Rachel Hauck, costumes by Alejo Vietti, lighting design by Kenneth Posner, and sound design and original music by John Gromada. The production stage manager was Davin De Santis. The cast was as follows:

SARAH	Diane Davis
BOBBY	Josh McDermitt
JACOB	Mark Blum
MAGGIE	Debra Monk
KATHY	Vanessa Aspillaga
AMY	Jamie Brewer

CHARACTERS

SARAH – married to Bobby

BOBBY – married to Sarah

JACOB – tightly wound and clenching to keep it that way

MAGGIE – unspooled and unspooling

KATHY – Italian-American, heavy New York accent, visibly pregnant, the walking embodiment of Long Island, New York

AMY – strong-willed woman with Down syndrome*

*Finding a talented actor with Down syndrome isn't difficult, so please do it.

Gail Williamson of *Down Syndrome in Arts & Media* is familiar with this play's casting needs and specifically represents talented actors with Down syndrome across the country.

SETTING

A plain room that is both nowhere and everywhere

TIME

Then and Now

AUTHOR'S NOTES

A slash (/) indicates overlapping dialogue.

An ellipsis (...) as its own line indicates an impluse that wants to be articulated but isn't.

My aunt Amy was loud and funny. She loved movies, Michael Jackson, the Hulk, and calling people "meatball." Her favorite restaurant was Friendly's. When she said to a waiter, "I'm hungry as a horse," they'd often look back confused because to an ear unfamiliar with her specific speech pattern it sounded more like, "You're my whore!"

Amy was born with Down syndrome during a time in this country when medical professionals told my grandparents they'd just given birth to a "Mongolian idiot" who would never learn to read, write, or possibly even sit up on her own. My grandparents followed medical advice to place her in a state-funded institution. Amy went on to accomplish all of these things, and though my family would visit and take Amy home for holidays and vacations, we were never a part of her life on a daily basis.

After she passed away, I was left with more questions than answers about my family's relationship with Amy and decided to write a play about that. I contacted an agent who specifically represents talented actors with Down syndrome. She connected me to Jamie Brewer, who I met when she was in New York...walking in fashion week. Spending only an hour with Jamie completely changed what I believed people with Down syndrome were capable of, despite having known my aunt my whole life. I left that meeting promising to write Jamie a play.

As we considered who we could cast as Jamie's understudy, I reached out to the same agent but this time didn't specify gender. The result was a lunch meeting with the actor Eddie Barbanell. Despite being told not to prepare anything, Eddie performed Romeo, Julius Caesar, and Puck over ice cream... I knew that he, too, had to be part of this play.

I went to Roundabout with this conundrum – how would we include Eddie when the title role was named after my aunt? The solution: writing a male version so both Eddie and Jamie could be a part of our production, and future productions of the play would be more inclusive, giving actors of both genders a title role.

I'd encourage future productions of this play to do the same and find ways, both with this production and with others, to be more inclusive of differently abled actors and audience members.

– Lindsey Ferrentino

Special thanks to Jamie Brewer, Edward Barbanell, Josephine Eilbacher, the teachers at the Cook Center Grammar School, and my family.

For my aunt Amy Jacobs
who is missed both for who she was and for who she could have been.

1.

SARAH. This is good! This is *good*, right?! You're having a good time?!!

BOBBY. Sarah –

SARAH. This is. In fact. Great!

BOBBY. Great!

SARAH. ...We have to start sitting. Were you even listening to the speaker? Come sit across from me. Sit with me please.

BOBBY. – on the floor?

SARAH. Please don't make me beg to start this.

BOBBY. – Indian style?

SARAH. What?

BOBBY. If we're sitting Indian style, I shouldn't have worn these tight pants.

SARAH. You think I care how you sit?

I told you not to wear slacks.

The brochure said dress comfortable. You look like you're going to a funeral. – Didn't you wear those pants *to* your father's funeral? You were all puffy then –

BOBBY. Sarah.

I am sitting in front of you.

SARAH. ...

...

And we're – supposed to. Look each other in the eyes –

BOBBY. ...

SARAH. – and repeat the facts of our life.

Until we believe them.

BOBBY. ...

SARAH. ...

BOBBY. ...

SARAH. Go.

BOBBY. I am – a man...

    I prefer to be a *quiet* man.

SARAH. Yeah, good, I'm a woman... See?! This is easy!

BOBBY. I am...a man.

    And.

    I am looking at my wife.

SARAH. *(Bursts into tears.)* ...

BOBBY. – no, no, what? Already?

SARAH. I'm not, / no –

BOBBY. – hey, hey, hey / don't –

SARAH. It's okay for – I'm looking at you too. That's what I'm doing.

    ...Your turn again.

BOBBY. I have an erection.

SARAH. Would you stop it.

    Talk about something Nice –

BOBBY. That *is* Nice. I'm looking at my wife and have an erection, that's a *compliment* –

SARAH. Talk about your job.

BOBBY. *(??)* My *job* is not nice.

    I have some *random* job when you're a kid you don't realize is an option.

       (Beat.)

SARAH. I don't – have one. Anymore.

BOBBY. – what?

SARAH. You're not supposed to comment, you're supposed / to keep going.

    You have a job, I don't, you go –

BOBBY. You just told me you lost your job – and I'm not supposed / to –?!

SARAH. – your turn.

BOBBY. Uh, I. Work for the electric company.

He fired you?

SARAH. I recently quit.

BOBBY. You – *what?*

SARAH. Eight months ago. Your turn –

BOBBY. I have a dog named Sam – I'm sorry, but *what the fuck* are you talking about?

SARAH. I – *also* have a dog named Sam.

Your turn.

BOBBY. That – that does not get to count. Could we skip / to –

SARAH. I'm not answering / until you give me back a fact.

BOBBY. Let's just get to what we came here for.

I enjoy chicken!

Your turn.

SARAH. After the baby, I never showed up to work again.

BOBBY. – what do you do all day when the kids are with my mother?

SARAH. Your turn...

BOBBY. ...I wear a size large shirt.

SARAH. – you don't, you wear an extra large now.

BOBBY. No –

SARAH. I've even bought you double-X sometimes, in the / nicer brands –

BOBBY. No, that's not, that is not / true –

SARAH. You're wearing a double-X, right now. Your turn.

BOBBY. ...

I am not.

SARAH. ...

BOBBY. *(Reaching for the tag.)* I can't see –

(Ripping shirt off.)

...There's not even a tag –

SARAH. I – cut the tags out when I buy you double-X.
When your shirts don't have tags, that's why.
Your turn.

BOBBY. ...You make me feel bad.

SARAH. ...

...Your turn.

BOBBY. That *was* my fact.

SARAH. It should be more like – On our first date, we went to the movies.

BOBBY. ...*I'm starving*. Do we get a lunch break?

SARAH. Put your shirt back on before you start talking about food, please.

BOBBY. Jesus, Sarah – how come I have to put my shirt on?

SARAH. *Starving* is not a fact of your life. That is a fact of *some* people's lives, but clearly not a fact of yours. I have mints in my purse, help yourself.

BOBBY. I'm *hungry*, I don't have bad breath!

SARAH. We are staying at a hotel with a free continental breakfast, but you couldn't even get out of bed early enough –

BOBBY. Sarah.

SARAH. We're at a couples retreat to help us *communicate* and this morning, I'm standing ALONE in front of the waffle maker – / *by MYSELF*.

BOBBY. Okay.

Ooo-kay –

SARAH. I'll get you the mints.

BOBBY. I can do / it –

SARAH. You'll never find them in there –

You put your shirt on.

BOBBY. ...

SARAH. Put your *shirt*.

BOBBY. ...

> *(She throws a mint at him. It bounces off his bare skin.)*

SARAH. Your constant eating these days disgusts me.

BOBBY. ...

SARAH. Here, I knew you'd get hungry. – Like packing for our son.

> *(She throws a banana at him. It bounces off his bare skin.)*

I'm sorry, the analyst here thinks if you'd take me into your arms –

BOBBY. *"Take you into my arms"?*

SARAH. – it would help overcome your frustration, which drives you to eat.

BOBBY. We came here to make a pretty major decision, I don't really think my snacking habits have anything to do / with it –

SARAH. He said what'd help is – if, when you crave a snack, instead, *embrace* me.

> *(**BOBBY** looks at her. Picks up the banana, peels and eats it.)*

> *(She throws more and more mints and a handful of change.)*

Fine, you know what, I don't / care.

BOBBY. I am trying to make you *laugh.*

SARAH. He also says hold hands when we fight. Because couples can't yell when they're touching –

BOBBY. I'd try *touching*, gimme / your –

SARAH. Oh, stop it. Stop. You stop it! Your turn –

BOBBY. I LIKE THE WAY I LOOK!

SARAH. I don't.

Yours.

BOBBY. – when did you stop liking how I look? Or you mean you don't like the way *you* look since the baby? Because I do. Still. A lot. *I like the way you look –*

SARAH. *(Softening.)* That's not really a fact.

BOBBY. Then how about we skip to why we picked our daughter's name –

SARAH. Do not – **DO NOT TALK ABOUT THAT YET.**

...

BOBBY. ...

SARAH. ...

BOBBY. *I don't know what you want.*

SARAH. That's why we're here. To figure it out!
With *facts* – that can't be disputed.
That's what we are *paying* to be / here for –

BOBBY. Our credit cards are well / aware –

SARAH. *Put your shirt on –*

BOBBY. Take yours off.

SARAH. ...

BOBBY. ...

SARAH. ...

BOBBY. You dress in the bathroom now.

SARAH. ...

BOBBY. I can't remember the last time you dressed with me
in bed –

SARAH. YOU'RE ALWAYS SLEEPING!

BOBBY. Take it off.

SARAH. No.

> ...
> You're being.
> No!
> This is.
> What if someone – /
> No.

BOBBY. They said nobody'll come in until we want them to.
Was the same when we got that massage on our
honeymoon. They don't say, "Hey use this room for sex,
but –"

SARAH. Oh *god.*
You think everybody does that?

BOBBY. You think we were the first?

SARAH. Oh, I hope they clean it.

BOBBY. ...

SARAH. ...

BOBBY. You know, I miss the days when you didn't "officially" wake me up. You'd just start *talking*. Asking me should you wear this. Did I pick up milk. You'd walk around in your bra or your underwear or no bra or no underwear or a shirt and some underwear, but you'd just be *talking*. Like we were *continuing* something from the day before –

SARAH. Stop –

BOBBY. *Now* –

Even today, you squeeze into that bathroom.

That RIDICULOUS hotel bathroom. /

You come out fully dressed.

And say, "COME ON. GET UP. HELLO, Bobby. UP, GOOD MORNING."

SARAH. *Stop* –

stop, **stop!**

We need to get back to / the exercise –

BOBBY. Take it off.

Please.

You wanna talk about this?

Then I am *begging* you to do this first.

This – is a thing that's apparently happening right now.

I am begging my own wife to take her shirt off.

Take that shirt off, Sarah.

SARAH. ...

BOBBY. *Take your shirt off.*

> *(Lights shift.)*
>
> *(Let it be weird and confusing because right now – it is.)*
>
> *(Something to jolt us to the present, like loud airplanes on the runway.)*

2.

(Greetings from across the airport.)

(Suitcases. Hugs. Real tight ones. **MAGGIE** *and* **JACOB** *embrace; old familiar rhythms, rapid-fire.)*

*(***MAGGIE*** *finishes a banana.)*

*(***JACOB*** *talks with his hands covering his mouth.)*

MAGGIE. *SO* good, *SO* good to see you, I miss my brother *SO* much.

Stop staring at how fat I got! I'm wearing layers.

JACOB. I'm not! / Come here.

MAGGIE. *SO good.*

JACOB. Almost missed my connection –

MAGGIE. Airport's a FUCKING zoo!

JACOB. Were you waiting long?

MAGGIE. Eh, I was dealing with a client. Then got our rental car 'til those traffic dicks made me keep circling.

JACOB. I have to get my bag – Where's carousel eight – I only see letters – Do you see any numbers?

> *(***MAGGIE*** *notices his hands, hits them away from his face.)*

MAGGIE. You a rapper now? Put your hands / down –

JACOB. I am itching my nose.

MAGGIE. Something happen to your mouth?

JACOB. Alright. Here. Fine.

> *(Shows off his mouth.)*

I have. I got braces. They're *braces*, okay?

MAGGIE. Braces?! ...Why.

JACOB. What do you mean, *why* – to straighten my teeth?

MAGGIE. You are sixty years old!

JACOB. Yeah, I'm *sixty*, I'm not Dead!

(Beat.)

Mom and Dad never did it for me and I can finally afford them.

MAGGIE. *(Laughing.)* Look what you look / like!!

JACOB. Stop laughing – *I have quite a serious jaw misalignment.* Are you – DO NOT TAKE A PICTURE OF ME RIGHT / NOW?!

MAGGIE. I have to post this to my social medias.

JACOB. Maggie, delete that, DELETE!!

MAGGIE. You're really not used to the way you look by our age? My last birthday I decided I'm eating how I want. Letting my hair gray. I do nothing, but snack like I'm from Spain.

JACOB. What?

MAGGIE. Tapas. All the time. Life is a constant stream of hummus to my face.

JACOB. Well. Not me. Diane and I, I'll tell you, we can*not* stop juicing. I'm so bad, we juice six times a day! Packed the whole set-up with me to juice for Amy.

MAGGIE. You're gonna deliver Dad's eulogy with those in your mouth?

JACOB. I'll get them off first.

MAGGIE. Oh good.

JACOB. That was sarcasm, Maggie. I am not bringing my orthodontist to Dad's *wake.*

MAGGIE. ...

JACOB. ...

MAGGIE. *(Sobbing.)* We are such shitty children.

JACOB. – we are *not* children.

MAGGIE. We should have *BEEN* there!

JACOB. *Been there?* Dad wasn't dying. He just *died.*

MAGGIE. *I* couldn't, I have my *clients* –

JACOB. Stop calling them clients, you're a real estate agent.

MAGGIE. *Well YOU* – you could teach middle school from anywhere – We should have *been* there –

JACOB. I would KILL MYSELF before I moved back to Long Island. I would commit suicide.

MAGGIE. We are *such* shitty children.

– aren't even children anymore – we're *orphans*!

We are ORPHANS now. We are ORPHANS, Jake.

JACOB. I HATE when people say that. We are not orphans. We had parents. They're just both *dead*.

MAGGIE. *(Sobbing.) Oh /* **GOD** –

JACOB. I'm sorry. Please wait to cry 'til we get to Mom and Dad's, / pull it together –

MAGGIE. – the worst! We're the worst –

JACOB. *(Looking around.)* – she's fine – seriously, she's, look away please, thank you – *Let's just – the carousel –*

MAGGIE. Why's it called a fucking carousel?!

JACOB. I think this is it – Is this eight?? I think this is eight. Why is nothing at LaGuardia properly marked?

MAGGIE. I'm gonna – I need to get this out of the way now.

...I can be honest with you 'cause we are *close*, right?

JACOB. Sure, yes, clearly very close.

MAGGIE. Good, so I am speaking my truth.

I cannot allow you to pull your new born-again-Christian bullshit at our Jewish funeral.

JACOB. – *I beg your pardon?*

MAGGIE. Like you did at Mom's.

My therapist is encouraging me to be proactive, this is me doing that –

JACOB. I wrote Mom's eulogy 'cause I'm the eldest –

MAGGIE. *Eldest.* – You Mormon now too? Elder Jacob over / here –

JACOB. You *asked* me to because you don't like talking in front of crowds!

MAGGIE. Oh come on, like you didn't sneak a fucking NEW TESTAMENT out after the rabbi.

JACOB. SNEAK?

MAGGIE. You pulled a tiny Christian BIBLE out of your pocket. That is something you literally did.

JACOB. – that was my pocket Bible – my pocket-sized Bible that fits in my POCKET!

MAGGIE. – you kept reading completely irrelevant scripture –

JACOB. – 'cause I couldn't find my place. It was a lot of pressure!

MAGGIE. Dad's JCC friends'll be there, we don't need anyone else to have a heart attack.

JACOB. *I just got off the plane.*

MAGGIE. And let me be the first to say no one's mistaking *that* face for a gentile's.

JACOB. – SO good to see you.

MAGGIE. …

Love ya, but I speak my truth.

JACOB. – oo-kay – we have a three-hour car ride if we don't hit traffic, which we will, so we don't need to plan Dad's funeral / this second –

MAGGIE. Dad was mortified by what you did at Mom's / and he's dead now.

JACOB. *(Mumbling.)* – wasn't mortified.

MAGGIE. He is dead now.

Dad is DEAD and we are ORPHANS!

JACOB. We are in an **AIRPORT!**

MAGGIE. …

JACOB. …

MAGGIE. …

JACOB. It's fine.

Let's just.

MAGGIE. This is good. This is good, right? This trip will be good. For both of us.

JACOB. What we need to worry about is how we're gonna tell Amy.

MAGGIE. ...

JACOB. ...

(*A horn that the luggage is coming.*)

MAGGIE. What's your suitcase look like?

JACOB. *(??)* – it's a suitcase.

MAGGIE. – could be *red*...or polka dot maybe –

JACOB. It's black. I own the same black rolling bag like every single person in America.

MAGGIE. – did you tie little pom-poms on the top, or –

JACOB. Do you *think* I tied little pom-poms on the top?

MAGGIE. ...You really should, Jacob. *You really should.*

JACOB. ...

MAGGIE. ...Is that it?

JACOB. No.

MAGGIE. ...

JACOB. ...

MAGGIE. ...Is that –

JACOB. Nope.

MAGGIE. ...

JACOB. ...

MAGGIE. ...That's –

JACOB. I'll alert you when it comes out.

MAGGIE. ...

JACOB. ...

MAGGIE. ...

JACOB. Do you remember Dad's friend Al? – With the ponytail and canes –

MAGGIE. I know *Al*! Of course I do! Al Schwartz has POLIO. *Who has polio anymore.*

JACOB. He called me to say we shouldn't bother having a funeral – nobody'll come 'cause all Mom and Dad's friends're dead too.

MAGGIE. Jesus, Jake.

JACOB. Al said it, not me!

MAGGIE. Well did you tell Al to go fuck himself –

JACOB. Yes, I told *AL-WITH-POLIO* to "eff" himself –

MAGGIE. This is our father. Whom we *love*.

JACOB. …There's just no point to have our kids flying around the country twice if we're gonna see each other for the Christmas –

MAGGIE. HANUKKAH!

JACOB. Don't start –

MAGGIE. Let's not have a funeral then! Why get him cremated?

JACOB. – ookay –

MAGGIE. When we could dig a big HOLE in the side of the Long Island Expressway, toss him in.

JACOB. Al said they stopped Tuesday poker games 'cause there's not enough players! Al's the last one, but he's not coming. Said the next funeral he goes to is his own.

MAGGIE. What do you suggest, Elder Jacob?

JACOB. Al – said – we should take Dad's funeral money, go to the movies and treat ourselves to a – *a Nice Steak at the Outback.*

MAGGIE. …God.

JACOB. *(Disturbed.)* …Dad told me Davey died *during* their poker game. Davey slumped over, cards still in his hand. Dad and Al called the ambulance – after the EMTs left, they – divided the dead man's chips. And kept playing.

MAGGIE. …

JACOB. No one'll come, Maggie

MAGGIE. *(Starts laughing or crying.)* Isn't there some *grown-up* who could take care of this for us?

JACOB. …I know.

I wish.

MAGGIE. …

JACOB. Look.

We are going to get in our rental car. We are going to pick up Amy as *quickly* as possible. And then, together, the three of us, will drive out to Montauk.

MAGGIE. How will we explain all this to Amy?

JACOB. ...I don't know. But we *will*, so we can get OUT of Long Island as fast as we can.

3.

(**KATHY**, *noticeably pregnant, talks to* **JACOB**.)

KATHY. *(Heaviest New York accent.)* – *Stove Top*.
I'm tellin' you.
Stove Top is THE brand. Last year our staff nurse Nancy asked if SHE could make the stuffing, had CLAMS in it, swear t'Christ – CLAMS, y'ever hear of such a thing?
CLAAAMS, with turkey? CLAMS! I say, "Is this a joke?" I'm sittin' at Thanksgiving here goin' – "Is this a practical joke, am I on candid fuckin' camera?" I'm sayin' t'myself. Whole group home smelt like Friday Bingo night at the rectory durin' Lent – like a **FUCKIN' FISH FRY!**

JACOB. Uh, sorry, do you know when Amy'll be back? We're in a teeny, *tiny* bit of a rush.

KATHY. Her work van should be back any minute.

JACOB. Yeah, could I have a cigarette if you don't mind?

(**KATHY** *digs one out of her giant purse but never stops talking.*)

KATHY. Every year I'm like MA why you gotta mix sausage in your stuffing, MA, lay off the SAUSAGE, you got high cholesterol, but my ma makes the best! So much better than Nancy-with-her-GADDAMN CLAMS. Ya like stuffing? Made Ma's recipe for the residents, they love it –

JACOB. – I'm a vegetarian.

KATHY. You are? But you're a MAN!

JACOB. Yeah, I'm a complete health nut, actually, gimme a light.

KATHY. Mine's not lit. Because if Susan thinks I'm givin' up smoke breaks 'cause a my baby, she's got another thing comin' –

JACOB. Hah, good idea!

KATHY. I'm full of 'em, lemme tell you. Spent my Thanksgiving at my dumb-ass boyfriend's – INSISTED on hosting. I say what can I bring? He says – "Kathy, bring y'*lasagne.*"

JACOB. *What are you talking about?*

KATHY. Exactly! You got it! I say, "*Lasagne?!*" – Dumb-ass boyfriend says, "Kathy, I'm makin' fancy raviolis." Like *don't offer* to host Thanksgiving if you got no respect for tradition. Don't ASK to be the one who brings stuffing then show up with some TV-Food-Network-I-live-in-Brooklyn-recipe made-a-GADDAMN-CLAMS-CASINO! Stove Top's what turkeys were put on Earth to be stuffed with. Am-I-right?

JACOB. – uh, stuff those turkeys.

KATHY. You the oldest sibling?

JACOB. Oh!

KATHY. Don't be insulted, babe. I have no idea how old you are.

JACOB. My whole life people said I looked young for my age.

KATHY. Who can tell with that metal mouth. You're like a big-ol-man-baby, throwing me off.

JACOB. *I have quite a serious jaw misalignment.*

KATHY. I have no idea how old you are.
  (*A pointed accusation.*) *I don't know you.*

JACOB. ...

KATHY. ...

JACOB. ...My, my sister's trying to find the group home director.

KATHY. Please. Susan don't work holidays. Me? I'm gettin' time and a *half*, I'm Kathy.

  (**MAGGIE** *approaches, balloons in hand.*)

MAGGIE. Cigarettes allowed on your little juice cleanse?

JACOB. – not a cleanse, it's a lifestyle –

(They look to **KATHY**.*)*

KATHY. Kathy-here, you prolly hearda me.

MAGGIE. Hi.

We are – Amy's *family*.

JACOB. She said Amy's work van'll be back any minute now. *Any* minute…

KATHY. You hear about Amy's big promotion?

MAGGIE. Of course we did, we're VERY involved.

JACOB. – 's great –

KATHY. – employee of the month August, October too –

JACOB. Really?

MAGGIE. October. I know. Of course I know that. Jake, I updated you.

KATHY. Amy's shift manager. Of one busy-ass movie theater.

MAGGIE. – we're so happy for her –

KATHY. – new boyfriend too.

MAGGIE. *We know.*

KATHY. Nick Nolte.

JACOB. Excuse me?

KATHY. – her boyfriend.

That's his name.

No connection.

Amy didn't tell ya? – Walks the halls goin' *Nick Nolte, Nick Nolte* –

You should see 'em together, we should be so lucky.

MAGGIE. We talk once a week.

KATHY. You and Amy?

MAGGIE. Me and Susan. She keeps me updated. Amy hates talking on the phone.

JACOB. Then Maggie passes everything to me, so.

KATHY. …Pff.

MAGGIE. …

JACOB. And we bought her these!

MAGGIE. Amy loves balloons.

KATHY. She won't like the Hulk balloon, she's not into him no more. And I don't know about the blue ones, red's her favorite color.

MAGGIE. She's my sister. I know what she likes.

JACOB. Pretty cold out, huh?

KATHY. Pfff!

Come January. You'd die. I'd pay to see that, bet you two'd actually die.

MAGGIE. You'd *pay* to see us *die*?

JACOB. – she's – / she's kidding –

MAGGIE. We're from Long Island originally. And we *have* come then, so.

JACOB. – you, uh, work here long?

KATHY. Pfff.

MAGGIE. Does. Does that mean a long time?

JACOB. Maggie.

KATHY. I DO practically run the place. Everyone's all, *Kathy*, what do we do? *Kathy*, where's the file, *Kathy*? Even Susan my supervisor's all, *Kathy*, you're the best at your job.

So I *know* your sister too.

MAGGIE. I take her to visit me in Chicago. For a week every summer, / I send those care packages.

JACOB. She's not saying anything.

MAGGIE. We send holiday cookie trays for the nurses – Legally, we are her primary caretakers.

KATHY. No, you're not. New York State is. Everybody here – New York's their ma, their dad, brother and sister too.

MAGGIE. ...

JACOB. ...

MAGGIE. I'm a contact, Dad was the *primary* contact, but I am also on the contact sheet. And this isn't our first time here. The three of us are *extremely* close. Tell her. Chime in ANY TIME.

JACOB. I. Both my siblings visit me in California. Every Christmas.

MAGGIE. *HANUKKAH!*

JACOB. We clearly have a great time.

> (**KATHY** *puts her hands up in peace, offers another cigarette.* **MAGGIE** *and* **JACOB** *both take one.*)

KATHY. Your sister loves talking to *me* on the phone, just so you know.

When I call t'get my hours. All the residents. *Kathy,* gimme Kathy they say.

Maybe you're not trying hard enough. Try again.

One week she'll love the Incredible Hulk, next week Hulk can kiss her ass. Fickle lady.

MAGGIE. – sweetheart though. Our Amy is so, so cute.

KATHY. *She is not a child.*

MAGGIE. ...

JACOB. ...

KATHY. She. LOVES my stuffing... – We blend it for the residents without good mouth structure, but there's some we didn't smoothie yet if you're hungry – long flight?

MAGGIE. We're fine.

KATHY. ...

Stove Top.

> (**MAGGIE** *puts her cigarette out into the Hulk balloon. It pops.*)

4.

*(In her room, **AMY** has headphones and excitedly watches a movie from an iPad, saying the lines along with the film.)*

KATHY. Her toothbrush, her dentures case is / here, PJs –

AMY. *(Movie.)* – **HAND IT OVER.**
DON'T FUCK / WITH ME!

KATHY. HEY!

AMY. Sorry, sorry – favorite part, Kathy. It's my favorite part.

> *(**AMY** holds an imaginary machine gun. Cheers. Mimes kicking something over.)*

KATHY. She won't pay attention to you 'til her movie's over.

AMY. *(Movie.)* – **POP THE REGISTER / OLD MAN!**

MAGGIE. Could she finish her movie in the car?

AMY. YOU THINK I GOT ALL DAY?!

KATHY. I'm packing her jeans, she doesn't have anything all black –

AMY. *(Movie.)* **HEY BITCH, YOU HAVE WAX IN YOUR EARS?! MOVE!**

JACOB. That's fine – HOLIDAY TRAFFIC, we should put a / move on –

AMY. *(Movie.)* **PAY ATTENTION TO THE GUN!**

KATHY. – coupla lil' Juicy Couture velour sweat suits, extra money on her government check has to get spent so we splurge –

MAGGIE. Where's her scrapbook – Amy and I made a scrapbook of her last visit to me.

KATHY. – have her name on it? Gotta Sharpie her name on everything here or how we supposed to know who's whose –

MAGGIE. I mean all photos pretty prominently feature her face.

KATHY. – haven't seen 'em, maybe / Nancy?

JACOB. Let's not –

KATHY. *(Shouting off.)* NANCY?!

JACOB. No, no, we need to go –

KATHY. NANCY SEE A PHOTO ALBUM??! / Lemme ask her – NANC-**AY!**

MAGGIE. We put it together – whole project, with stickers / and –

JACOB. We should, uh, hit the – hit the pavement.

AMY. *(Movie.)* **GONNA** *CRY* **NOW, LIL' DOUCHEBAG?**

JACOB. ...What. The HECK is she watching.

AMY –

MAGGIE. Kathy said her movie's almost over.

JACOB. CAN YOU SHUT THAT OFF / PLEASE?

AMY. *(Movie.)* **DROP THE GUN, YOU UNDER ARREST!!**

(**AMY** *mimes a big shoot-out battle.*)

JACOB. Amy, *please* – we need / to –

KATHY. Nance never hearda such a thing – Scrapbook? You sure –??

MAGGIE. Yes. Yes, / I AM sure.

AMY. *(Movie.)* **Thank you and GOOD NIGHT!**
Roll credits!

(**KATHY** *applauds and takes the headphones.*)

Thank you Kathy. Favorite part.

KATHY. Aim, your brother and sister are here for you.

MAGGIE. *(Smiling at* **AMY**.*)* ...

JACOB. *(Smiling at* **AMY**.*)* ...

AMY. *(Smiling at everyone.)* Uh...gimme a high five?

JACOB. Amy –

AMY. Down low?

(*As* **JACOB** *goes for it, she pulls her hand back and slicks it into her hair.*)

Too slow!
Loser.

KATHY. Hey babe, look, see what your brother and sister bought ya.

JACOB. Balloons, Amy!

AMY. *(Thumbs down.)* Booooooooooooo.

MAGGIE. Uh, come on, you love balloons. Remember I took you to that fair – she – she loved balloons.

AMY. I only love the color *red.*

MAGGIE. ...

JACOB. Let's HIT THE ROAD, JACK!

AMY. You, me?

MAGGIE. Yeah, a big road trip. Like in your movies.

AMY. You, me?

MAGGIE. You, me and Jake.

AMY. Jake's my brother though.

JACOB. Yes. He is. I am.

AMY. Kathy my friend.

KATHY. I'm your friend, that's right.

AMY. You, me, *Kathy.*

JACOB. Kathy-NO-NO-Kathy is absolutely *not* coming.

KATHY. Not to the service, of course, lemme grab my bag.

(**KATHY** *exits.*)

JACOB. Did she / just –

MAGGIE. Did we hear her wrong? We must have heard / wrong.

JACOB. Let's, *quickly* –

MAGGIE. Goin' home!

AMY. E.T. Phone Home.

JACOB. We don't have time for / that game –

MAGGIE. We have something to tell you about our father.

AMY. Luke, I am your father!

JACOB. Amy, pay attention, / okay –

MAGGIE. We're goin' home to Montauk.

AMY. Montauk where Burger King is.

MAGGIE. Yes –

AMY. And Mom and Dad.

MAGGIE. – yes –

JACOB. Maggie!

MAGGIE. Later – we'll explain it on the ride –

JACOB. Come with Jake now.

AMY. Forget it, Jake. It's Chinatown.

MAGGIE. What about me, Amy. You remember me?

AMY. Maggie's my sister.

MAGGIE. I'm your sister, that's right.

AMY. No. You are a very old lady.

MAGGIE. ...Oh.

AMY. I'm joking.

> (**KATHY** *re-enters.*)

KATHY. I call it my AFFAIR BAG 'cause I used it while I was having an affair!

JACOB. Uh –

MAGGIE. Sorry, are you going somewhere too? / Or –

KATHY. Montauk here we come –

AMY. *(Chanting.)* Montauk! Montauk! Montauk! Jake, Maggie, Kathy, / Amy! Jake, Maggie, Kathy, Amy!

MAGGIE. JACOB!

JACOB. Oh, I mean.
(To **AMY.***)* Kathy doesn't need to. That's why we flew into LaGuardia –
(To **KATHY.***)* To pick her up / and –

KATHY. Recent statewide policy change. She can't go unaccompanied.

MAGGIE. She is NOT unaccompanied, she's with her *family* –

AMY. Jake's my brother though –

MAGGIE. Amy, please tell her you're fine to go with us.

JACOB. – yeah, it's no / problem –

KATHY. State. Wide. Policy. Change.

The state requires Amy to be accompanied by a guardian. That'd be *me*. Or any other legal caretaker. The state covers travel expenses, food, / gas –

MAGGIE. What, you think we're not gonna *feed* her?

KATHY. I can no sooner release her to *you* than I could some stranger.

MAGGIE. ...

JACOB. ...

KATHY. I woulda driven her out east so you didn't hafta schlep through Queens –

JACOB. If that's true, why didn't anyone stop us from making these plans?

KATHY. Maybe Susan *assumed* you'd like to *see* where your sister lives.

MAGGIE. WE HAVE SEEN THIS PLACE BEFORE –

AMY. I have to call to say goodbye to Nick Nolte.

JACOB. Yeah, yes, sorry, Amy, of course –

KATHY. Be grateful she gets personal care here.
    I. Am a *Blessing*.

MAGGIE. I'm sure you are.

JACOB. Should we talk about this / outside –

KATHY. Your dad signed off – it's done.

JACOB. ...He did *what*?

KATHY. Your dad had the choice to become her legal guardian again or this. About six months ago.

AMY. Dad's in Montauk.

MAGGIE. – why would Dad have –

JACOB. This is hardly surprising behavior from him –

KATHY. Amy woulda lost all benefits she gets as a ward-of-the-state if your dad took her back.
    Easier this way.

AMY. Mom and Dad in Montauk, right Jake?

MAGGIE. ...We should go –

AMY. I have to work.

JACOB. You're getting *bereavement* time, Amy –

AMY. What is that –

MAGGIE. We'll explain it on the way.

AMY. Jake, tell Carol my roommate to water my plants. And watch my Nick Nolte.

JACOB. Absolutely.

AMY. He can not kiss other girls.
Or hug other girls.
Or hold hands with other girls.
Or have little chats with other girls.
Or look at other girls.
He can not see other girls with his eyes.

KATHY. That's right, keep your man on a short leash!

JACOB. ...Let's go. Everybody. Let's *EVERYBODY* go.

KATHY. I just – I have to be the one who drives.

MAGGIE. ...

JACOB. ...

AMY. *(To* **MAGGIE.***)* You my friend?

MAGGIE. – your sister. I'm your *sister.*

KATHY. No, it's a little game we play.

AMY. *(To* **KATHY.***)* You my friend?

KATHY. – of course I'm your friend.

AMY. *(Like she's scored a point.)* Yes!
(To **MAGGIE.***)* You my friend?

MAGGIE. – sure, I'll be your friend.

AMY. YES!

KATHY. And Nick Nolte's your friend?

AMY. YES!

KATHY. And Carol's your friend? And Susan's your friend?

AMY. Yes! YES!

JACOB. And Jake's your friend too!

AMY. No! Jake's my brother.
Enough.

KATHY. I'll get her changed, see y'at the car. Two seconds!

MAGGIE. ...

KATHY. Promise, ya won't even notice me, I'm like a little mouse. I'm real quiet and I eat A LOTTA CHEESE.

AMY. *Hasta la vista, baby.*

5.

(**JACOB** *and* **MAGGIE**, *by the car.*)

JACOB. HOW have we not left yet?? I pictured us landing. Picking her up *swiftly*. Getting on the road. Like a montage. Like a movie montage! Do you know what kinda traffic we're gonna hit?! THE TRAFFIC. Remind me not to die Thanksgiving weekend.

MAGGIE. Did you notice her wrist?

JACOB. Whose – whose / wrist –

MAGGIE. Amy's Caretaker. Kathy – has a tattoo of a big piece-a-fruit.
The Fuck do you think that's about?

JACOB. ...*I don't know.* WHO CARES.

MAGGIE. Oh it bears mentioning that the person the state's *entrusted* our sister to – is making some pretty questionable life choices.
– looks like a big fleshy vagina –

JACOB. Dear *Lord.* / Can you not –

MAGGIE. – all those seeds look like a *yeast* infection –

JACOB. There are enough reasons to hate that she's forced to come with us, I refuse to critique her self-expression –

MAGGIE. Self / expression –?!

JACOB. Maggie, let it go. Let this One. Thing. Go.

MAGGIE. I am not sitting next to her.

JACOB. This isn't her fault. It's Dad's.

MAGGIE. ...Don't.

JACOB. I will not pretend, now that he's *dead*, he was some perfect father figure –

MAGGIE. He was with you and me. And how he sat with Mom through the end –

JACOB. Growing up, we'd visit Amy *once* a month. If that.

MAGGIE. It was a different time, she was raised in very nice homes –

JACOB. On the rare trip to see her, where'd we go?

MAGGIE. – the movies.

JACOB. Exactly.

MAGGIE. I hate to ruin this "I-had-a-terrible-childhood narrative" you're always imagining, but the movies are a *normal* family activity.

JACOB. If you only see your daughter once a month, you might want to go some place you can actually *Talk.*

MAGGIE. ...

JACOB. ...

MAGGIE. Yeah. Well.

...Maybe that's why I was *hoping.* The *three* of us. Could *bond* on this road trip –

JACOB. Oh, stop calling it a "*road trip.*" This is Long Island, not the Grand Canyon!

MAGGIE. Be on my side for once.

JACOB. It's body art. It's a tattoo.

MAGGIE. *OF A FUCKING* **PAPAYA!**

> (**AMY** *and* **KATHY** *enter.* **AMY** *is dressed more like Kathy than* **MAGGIE** *and* **JACOB** *would like – the full Long Island special.*)

KATHY. Told you we wouldn't be long –

MAGGIE. Hi – Come! Come on in!

Amy, sit between us like when we were kids and we'd poke Jake 'til he'd cry –

JACOB. Yeah, how 'bout we don't do that.

Amy, sit with me so we can talk.

KATHY. Why don't we ASK Amy who she'd like to sit with.

AMY. I wanna drive.

JACOB. Good one!

AMY. People with Down syndrome CAN drive you know.

KATHY. Don't you start pullin' that card, miss.

AMY. Nick Nolte drives.

KATHY. Yeah, but you don't.

AMY. SHOTGUN!

KATHY. *(To* **JACOB** *and* **MAGGIE.***)* Keys, please.
You two.
In.

*(***JACOB** *and* **MAGGIE** *climb into the back seat.)*

JACOB. – this is really demoralizing.
You don't still get car sick, do you?

MAGGIE. I am an adult woman, Jake. *Please.*

*(***KATHY** *and* **AMY** *up front.)*

(Everybody's in.)

KATHY. Just get on the L.I.E.?

AMY. The L.I.E. is the World's Largest Parking Lot.

KATHY. Is it a pretty drive?

JACOB. Like everywhere else on Long Island. Mostly strip malls.

AMY. And Burger King.

MAGGIE. Our tradition is to buy Amy Burger King before we get off the exit, your favorite, right, Amy?

AMY. Two cheeseburgers. And *root-beer!*

JACOB. Be careful please, you're not on the insurance.

KATHY. Buckle up everybody. You buckled?

AMY. *(Showing off her wallet.)* This is my Nick Nolte.

MAGGIE. Aw, look at you two –

KATHY. …Here we go!…

JACOB. Get on the road, please!

AMY. YA – hooooooo –

MAGGIE. FAMILY TIME!

AMY. ROADDDDDD TRIPPPPP – YAAAA – HOOOOOO!

JACOB. YIPPEE!

AMY. YIPPEE-KI-YAY-MOTHER-FUCKER!

(Some definitive "road trip" starting climactic sound.)

(And they're off!)

(But then nothing much really happens. Because they're in a car. Onstage. And also, nothing ever happens on a road trip...except a lot of driving.)

KATHY. Lil' uh, traffic here.

MAGGIE. ...

JACOB. Great!

MAGGIE. That's alright!

We can still have a great time together.

We can, we can enjoy the sights!

AMY. Nail salon...

Bagel shop...

Nail salon...

GNC.

JACOB. That's right!

MAGGIE. – excellent reading skills, excellent.

AMY. Laundromat.

Dollar store.

Chili's.

Nail salon.

JACOB. Good job!

MAGGIE. This is good.

This is so good, right?

Amy, you're having a good time with us?

JACOB. We do really need to talk to you about something, about our parents.

MAGGIE. Can we have your full attention now, Amy?

AMY. Did you know *Aim* is my nickname.

My true friends call me *Aim*.

People you love call you a better name.

MAGGIE. Oh!

JACOB. I'm sorry, *Aim*?

AMY. You and Maggie should still call me Amy.

MAGGIE. ...

JACOB. ...

AMY. I don't wanna talk to you.

Can we have music?

Radio. Let's go.

> *(A song like "American Woman" by The Guess Who plays.*)*

---

*A license to produce *Amy and the Orphans* does not include a performance license for "American Woman." The publisher and author suggest that the licensee contact ASCAP or BMI to ascertain the music publisher and contact such music publisher to license or acquire permission for performance of the song. If a license or permission is unattainable for "American Woman," the licensee may not use the song in *Amy and the Orphans* but should create an original composition in a similar style or use a similar song in the public domain. For further information, please see Music Use Note on page 3.

6.

(**SARAH** *and* **BOBBY** *in stand-down.*)

(*He turns on the radio. A song like "American Woman" by The Guess Who plays.**)

SARAH. What're you DOING??

(*Volume up even louder. He dances, still shirtless.*)

BOBBY. I'M SURE THEY PUT A RADIO IN HERE FOR A REASON.

(*He dances, extends his hand.*)

(*She doesn't take it.*)

(*He dance-gestures that she should take her shirt off, swing it over her head, and throw it.*)

(*He sings the song on the radio at the top of his lungs.*)

SARAH. Oh my god, Bobby.
   – convenient lyrics.

(*Maybe this makes her laugh, but she's done. She grabs her purse. Heads out.*)

(*He dances more ridiculously, stopping her at the door.*)

BOBBY. Your shirt...
   No one's coming in.

---

*A license to produce *Amy and the Orphans* does not include a performance license for "American Woman." The publisher and author suggest that the licensee contact ASCAP or BMI to ascertain the music publisher and contact such music publisher to license or acquire permission for performance of the song. If a license or permission is unattainable for "American Woman," the licensee may not use the song in *Amy and the Orphans* but should create an original composition in a similar style or use a similar song in the public domain. For further information, please see Music Use Note on page 3.

(He takes her hair out of its pinning.)

(He takes her hands, places them on his bare chest.)

(They stare at each other, still.)

(She breaks away.)

(She picks up his shirt.)

(She puts it on top of hers.)

(In the way only women can do, she wiggles out of her own shirt – though she is still wearing his.)

(He applauds.)

(She drops her shirt. He catches it.)

(He tries to put on her shirt. He can't. Or maybe he can a little.)

(They dance.)

*(***BOBBY** *seals off the door with her shirt, lowers music, and reaches for something.)*

SARAH. What is that? What – are you buying drugs now?

BOBBY. No. Davey from poker, he *gave* it to me and Al.

SARAH. Al needs to cut off his ponytail and settle down.
I don't like this wild crowd you're playing poker with –

BOBBY. *Wild?* Al Schwartz has polio.

(They laugh. He reaches for a lighter, she stops his hand.)

SARAH. We shouldn't be acting like this is funny.
This is the most unfunny choice we've ever had to make.

BOBBY. *Facts*, Sarah –

*(***BOBBY** *sing-lip-synchs the song on the radio.)*

SARAH. I do want to.
Leave.

BOBBY. This room? Or –

SARAH. …

> *(She turns off the music.)*

I fantasize about it, like I'm testing myself.

Your turn –

BOBBY. …

SARAH. …

BOBBY. – don't – / why're –

SARAH. Your turn.

BOBBY. We're – too young for this.

SARAH. Since she was born, I'm *tired.*

BOBBY. Of course, she's a *baby* and we have two other kids – so all we do is fight now.

SARAH. We fight 'cause I'm tired of worrying we're not doing the right thing – it's sitting here, I'm sick 'cause I'm so tired of worrying and people staring at her, I need to think clearly / back up, BACK UP –

BOBBY. You said couples can't fight when they're touching…

> *(He takes her hand.)*
>
> *(He inches closer.)*
>
> *(He undoes the top button of her shirt.)*
>
> *(She starts to undo the rest.)*
>
> *(She is weirdly shy.)*
>
> *(He knows this.)*
>
> *(He turns away.)*
>
> *(She takes the shirt off.)*
>
> *(It drops to the floor.)*
>
> *(She wraps herself around his back.)*
>
> *(He turns her around.)*
>
> *(They cling to each other, touching as much skin to skin as possible.)*

SARAH. Tighter.

I don't want to breathe.

Tighter.

(Tighter. Tighter...)

BOBBY. Now what.

SARAH. ...Have you thought about Staten Island?

BOBBY. People from Staten Island avoid thinking about Staten Island.

SARAH. Don't joke, stop joking.

I've driven there and back, we could visit her on weekends.

BOBBY. When?

SARAH. We'll put the kids in the back, go visit her every weekend –

BOBBY. No, no, I'm asking when did you go...

I thought we were gonna go look together?

You already went?

SARAH. ...I've been touring those places...while you think I'm at work...

BOBBY. ...

SARAH. ...

BOBBY. ...

SARAH. ...

...Fact.

I like when your shirt's tight, here – it stretches, between your shoulders.

*(**BOBBY** inches his way closer to **SARAH**.)*

BOBBY. I – like when I stand next to you, we kind of overlap right – right –

(Touches her shoulder.)

...

SARAH. I like when we're at a party, you look like you're having a good time, but I know you're not 'cause your armpits are sweating.

(They laugh.)

BOBBY. You don't wanna leave.

Take that / back...

SARAH. Facts.

BOBBY. Our daughter's name means *love*. But that's not why we picked it. We picked it 'cause it was the shortest in that book of names. So even though the doctors told us she'll never learn to spell or write, if it was only three letters we said –

We –

We said we'd *try*.

SARAH. I *did* try – this has been me doing that. For you.

BOBBY. ...

SARAH. I will care for Jake and Maggie on my own if you don't wanna stay since I made this decision.

BOBBY. – since you've *made it*?!

SARAH. To be a good parent to one kid, we're not gonna be bad ones to two. I can't, I can't / do it –

BOBBY. I – I wanna live with you – I don't mean in a house. I mean, I wanna live my life next to yours. I've sort of been plannin' on that, Sarah?

SARAH. ...And you know what that / means –

BOBBY. Yeah, means I'll keep – going to your shitty parties with you.

Have opinions on your boss, tell you you deserve better.

If you're sick, I'll bring you ginger ale while you throw up.

And holidays –

I'll eat with your family, even the members I don't particularly like, so on our way home, we can make fun of them together.

SARAH. ...

BOBBY. I will – *hold you* when your people die.

I'll take pictures from our life together and nail them permanently into the walls of our house.

Our bodies will fall apart.

We'll lose our hair and teeth and our minds and we are going to get fatter. *Much* fatter. But we'll see each other every day, it'll happen little by little, so we won't even notice everything changing. And our whole life going by... Then we'll die.

And hopefully, our kids'll keep those pictures and say, *"Were they ever that young?"*

SARAH. ...

...I know I'm awful, but I can't – /

I can't –

BOBBY. Can't *what* –

Say it.

SARAH. ...

BOBBY. – but *you* need to be the first to say it, / just –

SARAH. We can't keep Amy.

We can't keep her.

7.

(**KATHY**, *to the audience.*)

KATHY. My dumb-ass boyfriend – he wants to host a big-ass baptism, we're not even married, but god forbid we miss *this* fuckin' sacrament!

So now we're pickin' godparents which is the sickest shit, you know, it's like *WHO outta you people will care for my baby if I can't.*

I'm like, "My best friend *obviously*." He's like, "Your best friend's a pothead." I'm like – "Well, point taken."

My dumb-ass boyfriend's got two sisters. One's happily married, big house, I'm like let's pick her, she cooks a good ziti and buys me gifts, but problem is – she already got kids of her own. Lemme tell ya, two kids, close in age, you got your hands full.

Then he's got this LOSER sister who nobody picks. Nobody picks her for anything. The good sister didn't pick her for either of her two kids, but my dumb-ass boyfriend's like, "*We gotta pick her, nobody picks her!*" I'm like, "There's a FUCKIN' reason *why!*"

She lives with your fuckin' father and take how she treats those dogs. Their dad watches dogs, ya know, for extra money. I dunno, he loves dogs. He's like – gay for dogs.

Well this asshole dog comes in the house, shits on the dad's sofa when the dad's not home. My dumb-ass boyfriend wants to hose it off, but the loser sister says we should leave the shit to teach their father a lesson. Lemme tell you this. It's HIS house. She don't pay rent. He takes in extra dogs to support his loser daughter and she's gonna let the dog shit ferment? Na, na, no. My dumb-ass boyfriend's draggin' the whole couch outside, gettin' the hose, she's screaming in the driveway, "*LEAVE THE SHIT ON THE CUSHION TO TEACH DAD TO RESPECT HIMSELF!*"

I'm all *yeah*, Rosario, if you think that's who I want to care for my baby, you're outta your goddamn mind.

– what're these, Slim Jims on sale? I'll take four. And fill her up on pump thirteen.

Oh god, what to do…

Look.

I'm not sayin' there are only bad people in the world.
'Cause there are a lotta good ones too.
And most of us in-between.

But as my dumb-ass boyfriend always says:
Beggars cannot be choosers.
If it ain't YOU raisin' that baby…
– who knows *what* you're gonna get.

8.

(Still on the Great American Long Island Expressway, everyone eating clearance Slim Jims.)

MAGGIE. The air vents aren't working. We're getting no air back here!

AMY. Kathy, it's your turn. Name game. Letter C.

KATHY. C I'm – Candylicious, my husband is named Chad.

MAGGIE. Candylicious –

KATHY. I DO know two people named that.

MAGGIE. Oh, I don't doubt it.

KATHY. We come from – *Canada*. To sell you – crack-cocaine. Double points.

MAGGIE. There's no points.

JACOB. I'll go!

KATHY. Letter D.

JACOB. D my name is – Darling Amy –

AMY. HEY THAT'S ME –

JACOB. We come from –
(Australian accent.) Down Under.

KATHY. Woah –

AMY. You're funny, Jake.

JACOB. *(Australian accent.)* To sell you Dingos.

AMY. A dingo ate my baby...

JACOB. Who's next – Maggie?

MAGGIE. *(Fanning herself.)* E my name is Ethel and my husband's name is Ed.

AMY. No, Maggie. You are divorced.

JACOB. Oh! / Uh –

MAGGIE. – honey, no, no – that's the game –

AMY. No, in real life. Your husband's no more, you are divorced!

JACOB. – they're, uh, only separated, Amy –

MAGGIE. We're – divorced actually, now.
   Happened before she came out last summer.

JACOB. You didn't tell me?

MAGGIE. Not like you call.

KATHY. I am SO SO sorry –

MAGGIE. – air vents working?

KATHY. Awful – divorce is TERRIBLE –

MAGGIE. Yeah, I'm aware.

AMY. Maggie, do not *lie* and say you're married!

MAGGIE. Let's MOVE ON –

JACOB. *Amy!*
   Your turn –

MAGGIE. – shitty rental, can't even get my fucking vents
   open –

JACOB. F your name is –

AMY. Amy.

JACOB. And your –

AMY. – boyfriend is Nick Nolte.

JACOB. Yes –

AMY. I come from Staten Island.

KATHY. – you live in Queens now, we try to remind her –

AMY. I COME FROM STATEN ISLAND.
   To sell you – nothing.

JACOB. Great!!

AMY. My Burger King – I see it, Jacob –

MAGGIE. We need to get out of this car.
   I'm gonna freak out if I stay in this car –

JACOB. I thought you don't get car sick anymore –

KATHY. You need a puke bag?

MAGGIE. Just pull over –

AMY. *(Chanting.)* Puking! Burger King! Puking! Puking
   Burger!

MAGGIE. I need to get outta this car, I think I'm gonna be –

AMY. I want cheeseburgers, french fries and root beer!

MAGGIE. Amy – Amy –

AMY. I want cheeseburgers, french fries and root beer!

MAGGIE. Don't talk about cheeseburgers – Oh god, I'm gonna –

KATHY. NOT IN THE CAR, HEY!

NOT IN THE CAR!

AMY. I WANT THE BIGGEST CHEESEBURGER EVER!!

(**MAGGIE** *vomits.*)

EWWWWWWWWWWW –

JACOB. Oh god –

Oh god, you know how I –

I'm a sympathetic vomiter.

(**JACOB** *gagging.*)

KATHY. Jesus Christ.

Hold it, I'm pulling in that parking lot!

MAGGIE. Put on the brakes.

Put.

On.

The BRAKES.

(*The car stops.*)

This is good, this is still good! Right?

KATHY. I'm taking Amy to order.

Here's wet naps and a trash bag.

Use 'em.

(**KATHY** *and* **AMY** *get out of the car and exit.*)

(**JACOB** *and* **MAGGIE** *go to exit as well but can't get the doors open.*)

JACOB. ...Child locks.

MAGGIE. – oh for fuck's sake –

(**MAGGIE** *squeezes into the front seat like she's passing through a birth canal.*)

(**MAGGIE** *opens the door for* **JACOB**.)

(They get out and clean.)

JACOB. ...

...

Are you – you're – you're doing fine, though?

MAGGIE. What?

JACOB. The divorce –

MAGGIE. Yeah, oh – it's – yeah, well until recently I had this *scare.*

My health, just my health, just a health scare.

JACOB. *What?*

MAGGIE. I found – a lump.

(Indicates chest.)

In my –

JACOB. Oh! Are you – oh my god –

MAGGIE. My first thought, I thought, I wanna call *Mom...* Then I wanted a husband, (not my ex – he's not gettin' near *these* again) but I would've liked someone in bed to check, I am supposed to HAVE that at my age. You and I are not close anymore. *Who did I have to call?!*

JACOB. Uh... A *DOCTOR*, Maggie, you kidding me? You call a doctor!

I'm not gonna fly across the country to give my sister a breast exam –

Did you go, did you have it checked? Did you call??

MAGGIE. I'm fine, it was a few / months ago –

JACOB. You need to / have that –!

MAGGIE. You're not letting me get to the point –

JACOB. Don't gimme yours and Mom's "we practice Eastern medicine" – but-we-don't-know-anything-about-Eastern-medicine-so-we-just-eat-organic-eggs crap, I'm calling Diane's practice –

MAGGIE. It wasn't a lump, okay? It was a Skittle.

JACOB. ...

MAGGIE. ...Turned out *just* to be a Skittle, alright, so drop it –

JACOB. ...

   ...

   A – *Skit-Tle.*

MAGGIE. I had been at the movies. Then fell asleep in my bra.

   – I said it was a *scare*!

JACOB. ...I am going inside!

MAGGIE. I'm saying the three of us, we are NOT close anymore.

JACOB. If you didn't act like movie theater candy melting into your bosom was stage four cancer –

MAGGIE. The three of us – at holidays is *not* good enough. We can't even catch up before the visit's over –

JACOB. That's why it is really –

   (Close.) "Fucked. Up."

   And I do not say that word anymore, you know, but you've driven me to it. It is quite truly. "Fucked." To mention *cancer* / after Mom.

MAGGIE. I was terrified. Only for a second, but I had NO ONE. My boys have moved *all over the place.* It was scary, then funny, I had no one to laugh with either 'cause I'm alone.

   I am actually – Alone.

   I don't see that changing any time soon.

JACOB. ...

MAGGIE. ...

JACOB. Have – have you been dating?

MAGGIE. Oh, shut-up.

   Take my vomit bag.

JACOB. You're a catch! Get on out there! If at first you – Try, try again.

   Or call me? Any time, day or night –

   The phone works both ways.

MAGGIE. ...

JACOB. ...

MAGGIE. People are not meant to live in a country this big.
Picking up Amy. We had to fly in. Drive the length of
Long Island, if we were in Europe, we'd be in – like,
fucking Germany by now.

JACOB. What?

MAGGIE. If we lost planes and phones, I'd *never* find any
of you.
Families should *not* be this spread out.

JACOB. ...

MAGGIE. Forget I said anything. It was a –

JACOB. A *Skittle.*

(*They kind of laugh.*)

MAGGIE. I have mints in my purse, hand me one?

JACOB. You sounded just like Mom –
(*Imitation.*) *I have mints in my purse, help yourself.*

(*They take mints, look toward Burger King.*)

MAGGIE. We need to go and tell Amy about Mom and Dad
already.

JACOB. Inside a Burger King?
Okay.
I'd like to do this together.
Will you do this with me?

MAGGIE. ...

9.

(Inside Burger King, **AMY** *and* **KATHY** *eating.)*

JACOB. Cool crown, Amy.

AMY. I eat barbecue, ketchup, honey on every french fry –

MAGGIE. Can I have one?

AMY. No.

JACOB. I forgot how fast she eats –

MAGGIE. – we –

Amy, your brother and I, need to talk to you.

(To **KATHY.***)* ...Do you mind?

KATHY. Oh, no, not at all...

MAGGIE. *(At* **JACOB.***)* ...

JACOB. She meant –

KATHY. Thank you. I know what she meant. But. I'm on the clock.

MAGGIE. ...

JACOB. ...

MAGGIE. Amy, can we talk to you?

AMY. You cannot have my fries, Maggie.

MAGGIE. No, I'm / *not* –

AMY. You cannot have my french fries. *Mine.*

JACOB. Amy, slow down, you'll choke.

AMY. Kathy, she steal my food! / She steal my food.

MAGGIE. I'm not / stealing –

KATHY. No one's stealing your food Amy.

AMY. MINE, MINE, MINE!

MAGGIE. Jake, care to help me out here?

JACOB. Amy.

Okay, uh, listen.

Pretend – these are...

This.

(Lines straws up on the table, end to end.)

This line...right here...

This is...all of time.

AMY. *(To* **MAGGIE**.*)* What?

MAGGIE. I have no idea.

JACOB. Picture hundreds and thousands and millions and billions of straws, more straws than you can *imagine*, in a line that –

This line goes on. And on – *forever*. Can you picture that?

AMY. Yes, Jacob.

JACOB. – that's: *Time.*

And

this –

> *(Rips the top of the straw wrapper.)*

– little piece here. Is about a hundred years –

– if you're lucky.

Usually less.

This.

Is – a human life.

AMY. No.

No, Jake, that's a *straw wrapper*.

JACOB. Yes, but no.

When someone reaches the – end of their life, this little piece, goes back into that big line.

And that – THAT is what has rather recently, unfortunately – happened to – both Mom and Dad.

AMY. ...?

KATHY. ...?

MAGGIE. Okay, you've actually lost *me* now.

JACOB. This! ...Is the beauty of Heaven.

MAGGIE. Alright, nope! NO, that's enough of that!

AMY. Jake.

Maggie.

This is a *straw.*

(Scrunches the straw wrapper to one end.)

AMY. But this – is a
worm.

JACOB. No, Amy –

AMY. Listen to ME.
Dad makes worms for me.
This –
is a
worm.
Watch… I teach you, watch –

> *(**AMY** takes a drop of water from her cup and
> drops it onto the "worm.")*

– this is a worm – growing.

…

Magic.

JACOB. No, Amy –
TIME!

> *(**AMY** blows the straws all over **JACOB**'s lap.)*

MAGGIE. I don't know, we'll have to try to tell her again at
the house.

> *(**MAGGIE** shoots a straw at **JACOB**'s face.)*

What do ya got there?

KATHY. Six bacon cheeseburgers, no buns –

MAGGIE. No carbs, nice –

KATHY. Gotta be healthy when you're eatin' for two.

AMY. Mom and Dad do not make worms no more.

JACOB. …

MAGGIE. …What?

> *(**AMY** makes a worm on the table.)*

AMY. Kathy told me
Mom and Dad
die now.

JACOB. Oh…?

MAGGIE. You already did?

KATHY. Of course. When you called yesterday.

And when you didn't invite her to the first funeral.

JACOB. ...

MAGGIE. ...

JACOB. ...We wanted Dad to feel better first –

(*To* **KATHY.**) – for the *three* of us to tell Amy together.

Our dad just died before that happened.

KATHY. Really none of my business.

I'm only here for Amy.

MAGGIE. *So are we.*

AMY. Mom dead. Dad dead too.

MAGGIE. *That's right.*

JACOB. Amy. Do you know what – *dead* means?

AMY. Jake...

Dead. Is.

When you die.

They *dead.*

Get it?

Like Sam our dog.

In the ground.

– gone.

They never go home.

Never say hi.

Dead is gone.

(**AMY** *gestures slitting her throat.*)

Get it?

No more.

No more.

I take these straws.

So I can do it now.

Or –

No worms for me.

(**AMY** *sticks the straws into her front pocket.*)

MAGGIE. ...

JACOB. ...

MAGGIE. ...You need a hug?

AMY. I need ketchup.

MAGGIE. ...You sure? It can be good to / hug –

AMY. You?

Need a hug, Maggie?

Or ketchup?

> (**AMY** *hugs* **MAGGIE.**)

MAGGIE. Tighter...

Tighter...

I don't want to breathe.

JACOB. There is a place, Amy...

Where all time and people and places exist in the same space...

When a life is over, it never leaves us.

The life moves back into that line that goes on and on and on...

> (*After a beat,* **AMY** *unsympathetically bites her cheeseburger over* **MAGGIE**'s *hug.*)

10.

(We shift to the retirement home.)

JACOB. Al said the coroner left Dad's jewelry and wallet on his nightstand. I'm gonna go check to make sure everything is there.

*(**JACOB** exits.)*

MAGGIE. ...Weird to be in here now, huh? So quiet.

AMY. Mom and Dad's TV is off.

MAGGIE. You're right. Should I turn it on for you?

AMY. No.

TV movies suck.

Kathy set up my iPad movies please.

KATHY. Maybe this is a time, Amy, you should go be with your brother and sister...

AMY. MOVIES Kathy.

*(**KATHY** sets a movie to play on Amy's iPad.*
***AMY** puts on her headphones and sits between*
***KATHY**'s legs so **KATHY** can braid her hair.)*

JACOB. *(Offstage.)* There's a jar of mustard on Dad's nightstand, why is there mustard?

MAGGIE. Obviously Dad ate a sandwich in bed before he passed, Jake?! Come sit with us!

KATHY. You should put together one of those memorial slideshows. Like to Sinatra.

MAGGIE. – yeah, maybe.

AMY. Movie not playing, Kathy.

*(**JACOB** enters.)*

JACOB. Everything's there, but his car keys.

MAGGIE. Dad always kept them in his back pocket.

JACOB. Oh *great*. That means his car keys are at the crematorium. Just great. Now I have to google a locksmith.

MAGGIE. Jake, it's okay. Come sit down.

JACOB. Al said the TV was on when the EMTs broke in.

I'm gonna check Dad's TiVo, I could probably figure out what time he died.

I'm gonna check the dishwasher to see if there's any plates with mustard on them because I don't understand why there's this little jar of mustard next to his bed!

KATHY. Your dad have trouble breathing?

JACOB. He was on oxygen –

KATHY. Huffing mustard helps clear passageways.

JACOB. You think our dad was "huffing mustard"?

AMY. Kathy, my movie – my movie will not play –

MAGGIE. I'd like for the three of us to take this moment *together*, Amy would you mind shutting that off so we can sort through Dad's things as a family.

JACOB. It's already boxed up in there.

MAGGIE. What?

JACOB. Staff here does a clean-up, so the family doesn't have to.

MAGGIE. It's *done*?

– even Dad's clothes?

JACOB. – donated.

MAGGIE. No –

AMY. Movie not playing –

KATHY. Alright –

MAGGIE. I thought we'd go through Dad's things together.

We'd cry and laugh and get into a big fight over his trinkets, that's the typical sibling experience.

I thought that you, me and Amy should at least get that.

JACOB. I don't know what to tell you.

MAGGIE. Let's pick out photos and plan Dad's memorial –

JACOB. No one'll come, Maggie. There isn't going to be one.

MAGGIE. We have NOT decided that –

JACOB. We'll do it at Christmas –

MAGGIE. HANUKKAH! For fuck's sake, we are good fucking Jews!!

> (**JACOB** *starts unpacking his suitcase.*)

What are you doing?

JACOB. You know how Dad food shopped. Look at all that valuable produce –

MAGGIE. You better not –

That *better* not be your little juicer, Jake.

JACOB. Maggie, my blood sugar's plummeting, I'm not gonna eat fast food like you and the rest of our family then complain how fat we are.

MAGGIE. Take your hands off our dead father's fucking fruit!!!

This is NOT.

This is not how this is supposed to go! This is not how I imagined it.

I'm getting the photos.

> (**JACOB** *juicing.* **AMY** *watching her movie.*
> **MAGGIE** *pushes in a few cardboard boxes.*)

KATHY. I'd love to see some of Amy –

JACOB. Good luck finding any.

You can't exactly bring a camera into a movie theater –

MAGGIE. Don't say that, Amy was around!

(To **KATHY**.*)* There are *plenty.*

KATHY. I didn't mean anything –

MAGGIE. Look, here she is right here, as a baby –

JACOB. That's me.

MAGGIE. ...Are you sure?

JACOB. Yeah.

MAGGIE. Well.

Bald then, bald again.

> (**MAGGIE** *searches.* **JACOB** *juices.* **MAGGIE** *keeps looking.*)

(To **JACOB**.*)* Of course *yours* are in albums.

I remember this orange shirt of Mom's –
Look at Mom and Dad.
Look how young they were –

(Searching.)

...

...

...Where is Amy...

KATHY. Eh, don't worry about it.

Same in my family.

Firstborn ya can't stop snappin' photos, the kids after that it's like – who are you again?

MAGGIE. Exactly!

JACOB. That is not what's going on here, Maggie, and you know it.

MAGGIE. Jake.

JACOB. Yeah, it was a "different time."

MAGGIE. Do not.

JACOB. Amy's listening to her movie, she can't hear –

MAGGIE. Amy was fine where she lived.

Yes, we coulda visited more, but we have done right as adults.

You know how many families don't go at all?

KATHY. ...Pff.

MAGGIE. Mom and Dad always said she preferred being with her friends.

KATHY. They said what?

MAGGIE. In Staten Island, she was the nurses' favorite.

KATHY. In Staten Island, she was in Willowbrook.

MAGGIE. ...?

JACOB. ...?

MAGGIE. ...

JACOB. ...

KATHY. Most kids were stuck in pens all day, nobody changin' diapers, not enough clothes?

MAGGIE. ...

JACOB. ...

MAGGIE. ...No, that's ridiculous!

JACOB. What?

KATHY. There were *seventy* residents per caretaker. Why do you think she eats so fast? She *had* to.

MAGGIE. ...She.

No.

She was in a group home in Staten Island, but I would have known if she was *there*!

KATHY. Haven't you ever noticed a chunk of her leg's missin' from frostbite?

She was left outside during a blizzard.

JACOB. What?

MAGGIE. That's – no, she's – no, that *cannot* be true –

KATHY. You never wondered why she's got dentures?

Her teeth rotted 'cause, for a year, she was fed dog food.

Amy's a member of the Willowbrook class – kids in this country raised by the state didn't develop not 'cause a their disability, but 'cause of abuse.

We dunno what she coulda been capable of.

MAGGIE. ...

Jake...

Jake, tell her – Mom and Dad would not have allowed, they wouldn't have –

JACOB. And we would have known!!

MAGGIE. They would not – They would NOT have / allowed –

JACOB. Maybe, maybe Mom and Dad weren't told...?

KATHY. Of course they were. Those places were busted open, all over the news.

Wait, you two really didn't know?

JACOB. We knew she was in group homes her whole life, but – when we'd pick her up, they'd always have her ready to go, outside.

KATHY. Her records are not secret.

   …

   But you woulda had to *Ask*.

   (Silence.)

   (More silence.)

JACOB. Why did they never tell us?

MAGGIE. How did they not – Jake, how did they not take her back??

KATHY. Listen, Amy's been in good hands for *years*.
   Home cooking, Ma's stuffing. As *much* as she wants.
   She can't even remember –

MAGGIE. Thank god.

JACOB. – we can't have it both ways, Maggie.
   That means she also may not really remember *us*…

MAGGIE. …

JACOB. …

KATHY. …

AMY. Willowbrook is in Staten Island.

JACOB. …What?

KATHY. …?

AMY. Willowbrook is in Staten Island. I always remember.
   I *come* from Staten Island, New York.

KATHY. Were – Amy, were you –
   Were you listening?

   (**AMY** *takes her headphones off.*)

AMY. I told you. Movie not playing, Kathy.

MAGGIE. …

JACOB. …

MAGGIE. …

KATHY. …

   (An abrupt, unwanted lights shift.)

11.

(Kim Wu's Chinese Buffet and Take Out.)

(From a boombox, the finale of a song like Frank Sinatra's "My Way" blares tinnily on top of the already-playing Chinese restaurant music.*)

*(**MAGGIE** steps forward with a microphone.)*

*(**AMY** plays with the straws.)*

MAGGIE. Thank you *everyone* for coming to Mom and Dad's favorite restaurant for our memorial. Thank you to Kim Wu's Chinese Buffet and Take Out for this back room and this Radio Shack karaoke machine. My apologies to the staff – for my gross over-estimation of our party size. Please enjoy the crab rangoons, which were Dad's favorite. We placed *twenty* orders – that's one hundred and sixty crab rangoons. So please. All THREE of you. Eat your heart out.

JACOB. Maggie, I don't really think the microphone is entirely necessary –

KATHY. They really *are* delicious.

MAGGIE. Thank you. Thank you Kathy. They *are*. Raise a glass to Kathy, everyone!

AMY. To KATHY!

MAGGIE. And for this *Mai Tai*, cheers to Kim Wu!

AMY. To Kim Wu!

---

*A license to produce *Amy and the Orphans* does not include a performance license for "My Way" or any "Chinese restaurant music" under copyright. The publisher and author suggest that the licensee contact ASCAP or BMI to ascertain the music publisher and contact such music publisher to license or acquire permission for performance of the song. If a license or permission is unattainable for "My Way" or any "Chinese restaurant music" under copyright, the licensee may not use the song in *Amy and the Orphans* but should create an original composition in a similar style or use a similar song in the public domain. For further information, please see Music Use Note on page 3.

MAGGIE. Amy, we're here to remember our father Bobby; a navy war vet who liked to cook, was devoted to one marriage, had three kids...

Our parents. Loved us.

All of us. You know that Amy?

JACOB. – okie, dokie –

MAGGIE. Remember Amy, how we'd pick you up every Christmas, and our Jewish parents would take us to this Chinese buffet. Before Jacob met his shiksa wife so quit drinking to find juicing and Jesus Christ – Do you remember??

AMY. *Cheers* to Jesus Christ!

JACOB. Can we be serious, I too would like to say a few things.

MAGGIE. I feel a prayer coming on –

JACOB. There's / something *else* I'd like to –

MAGGIE. We want a prayer. We want a prayer. / We want a prayer. We want a prayer –

AMY. *(Repeating.)* Prayer, prayer, prayer, prayer!

>(**MAGGIE** *puts the microphone to* **JACOB***'s face. Microphone squeak.* **JACOB** *raises his hands to praise.*)

JACOB. Thank you oh Lord for the foods we are about to receive.

That my siblings have already started receiving.

In the good lord's name, we pray.

Amen.

AMY. Amen!

JACOB. Amy.

In honor of Mom and Dad –

And to make amends –

MAGGIE. I thought we were doing this later?

JACOB. This should have been done *years* ago.

I want to say, I want you to know, Amy, I have worked my whole life to – to separate myself.

From Mom and Dad.

I am NOTHING like them.

I am NOTHING like our parents.

So, Amy –

With my girls going to college, I just spoke to Diane, and well we'd – like to welcome you.

Into our home.

AMY. What?

JACOB. We'd like you to come live with us.

MAGGIE. Amy, when your parents die, that's the end of siblings being bound together by obligation. It's on US now. And we don't take that lightly.

JACOB. I'd like for you to come to California –

MAGGIE. Or Chicago –

AMY. At Christmas, Jake?

To get my presents?

JACOB. No, Amy, well, no – for – much longer.

AMY. 'Til New Years?

JACOB. Diane and I would – love for you to *live* with us, Amy. In our house.

In our home.

KATHY. …This, I did not see coming.

MAGGIE. Amy, Jake and I want you to live with one of *us* now. To *choose* which one of us you wanna live with.

AMY. – for how long?

MAGGIE. For.

For your whole life.

KATHY. Are you f'real?

MAGGIE. Forever!

AMY. Forever is.

In December for presents.

JACOB. *(Getting his straws.)* No, uh, Amy. This – is *Time.*

KATHY. Sorry, I don't mean to ruin this beautiful moment here, touching really, but did you talk to Susan?

JACOB. Well, we will –

KATHY. She'll lose all state benefits –
She has an important *routine*.

AMY. Sing-along Wednesday.
I work at the movies.
I clean the butter machine.
Monopoly Sundays.
Then family dinner.
Right, Kathy?

JACOB. We'll do that too.
At my house, every night is family dinner, Amy.

AMY. With Nick Nolte?

JACOB. Oh –

AMY. Nick Nolte comes to family dinner.
Right, Kathy?

KATHY. California's a long commute –

AMY. *What?*

MAGGIE. You'll have your own room at my house – no
roommates –

AMY. *No Carol?!?*
Where will Carol be?!

JACOB. I've – taken you to those top-of-the-line movie
theaters, how 'bout those reclining seats?

AMY. ...I do like movies.

JACOB. So – is that a yes?
You want to live with Jake?

MAGGIE. Or Maggie. I'd love the company.

JACOB. Amy, with Mom and Dad gone, there's no reason
for you to stay in New York anymore.

AMY. ...
But.
I *live* here.

JACOB. But –

AMY. But –

I live *here.*

Here.

My bed.

My blankets.

My clothes, my iPad here.

JACOB. We would, of course, help you pack –

AMY. My job.

The movies here.

Nick Nolte. Nick Nolte here.

Roommate Carol – here.

Susan –

Nancy –

Nacho, Bonnie, Albert here.

You don't even know their names.

MAGGIE. Amy –

AMY. Kathy. Kathy here, Kathy *not* in California.

Mom and Dad here, but they die now.

But Amy is alive – here.

Here I *STAY!*

JACOB. Where are you going?

AMY. I need to please use the bathroom, please.

KATHY. I'll come with you –

AMY. NO – I need to please use the bathroom please –

KATHY. Okay, I'm –

AMY. My*self.* I going myself.

MAGGIE. Can / we –

AMY. Myself!

I can go to the bathroom MYSELF.

MAGGIE. It's fine.

Okay, Amy. Go –

(**AMY** *runs out.*)

KATHY. I'll give her a minute alone, then go check on her –

(**BOBBY** *and* **SARAH** *enter.*)

SARAH. When you see Willowbrook –
> There are these big trees out front, green lawns.
> Brick buildings, looks more like a college campus –

BOBBY. That isn't –

SARAH. And you know what everyone says is best for her.
> And for us.
> And for our other two kids.
> From the doctor to our parents to our rabbi.
> What every single person has –
> Don't make me say it again.

BOBBY. Tell me how we're supposed to do this –
> You need to tell me.

SARAH. We.
> Put on our clothes...
> Get the keys.
> Leave this room.
> Drive home.
> Tell the kids.

BOBBY. Tell them *what.*

SARAH. Pack her diapers and her little clothes.
> Find someone to take the crib, 'cause we are *not* having
> another and I can't, I can't see it in the house –
> Drive, drive to Staten Island.
>
> Drive back –
> Sit with each other.
> Knowing what we did.
> Year after year –

KATHY. What is taking her so long –
> I'll go check –

BOBBY. But – I know you, Sarah.
> I *know* you...
> I have – from, from when we met –

SARAH. You are sleeping.
> All the time now.

You are eating.

Constantly.

I can't get you outta bed.

BOBBY. ...We are *good* people –

SARAH. Bobby.

...

...

You barely pick her up.

*(Quite suddenly, **SARAH** crosses the room.)*

(And picks up her shirt.)

(And puts it on as quickly as possible, unable to look at him.)

(She hands him his.)

*(**BOBBY** looks back at her, devastated.)*

(He puts it on.)

KATHY. She's not in the bathroom –

JACOB. What?

KATHY. She ran straight out – Come, come on!!!

MAGGIE. Oh my god –

JACOB. AMMMMMMMYYYYYY–

(Traffic.)

*(Cars whizzing by. **AMY** emerges from the chaos downstage. Honking. **AMY**'s hair is blown.)*

MAGGIE. Oh my G– JAKE – she's on the median!

JACOB. Amy – Don't – DON'T MOVE!!

*(**AMY** steps forward. **MAGGIE** screams.)*

AMY. Maggie, Jake –

MAGGIE. Stay right there!

AMY. Stay, Maggie – Jake. I stay.

I STAY

I STAY

I STAY!

(**AMY** *goes to step off the median.*)

MAGGIE. DON'T!!

AMY. I STAY
I STAY
I STAY!!

MAGGIE.	**JACOB.**
Okay!!!	Yes –

AMY. Staying.

JACOB. Yes, / okay.

AMY. *Staying.*

MAGGIE. Yes, okay – it's fine, / you stay –

JACOB. You can stay.

KATHY. I got ya, I got ya, I got ya –

(**KATHY** *goes to* **AMY**, *helping her off the median.*)

BOBBY. We need to get out of here, already

JACOB. I'll go – I'll go pay the bill.

SARAH. ...You still hungry?

BOBBY. ...

SARAH. We can – pick something up? – On the way.

BOBBY. ...

SARAH. Bobby...?

BOBBY. What.

SARAH. ...Fine.
Forget it. I'll pick.

(*Beat.*)

KATHY. Let's get in the car, Amy.

(**BOBBY** *and* **JACOB** *pat their pockets simultaneously.*)

BOBBY. Do you have the –

JACOB. Where are the keys?

MAGGIE. They're in your back pocket.

SARAH. Keep them in your back pocket so you don't lose
   them.
   Come on. It's gonna be a long ride home.

   (All at once and all together:)

   *(**AMY** takes **KATHY**'s hand.)*

   *(**SARAH** takes **BOBBY**'s hand.)*

   *(**JACOB** puts his hand on **MAGGIE**'s back.)*

   (Everyone steps forward.)

   *(**SARAH** and **BOBBY** come together and open
   the door to unending bright light.)*

12.

(Icy, cracked sidewalks in Queens.)

(The present-present. The kind of late afternoon winter timelessness where you can see your breath and you're cold and uncomfortable and wondering where the day has gone – where it's too late to do anything and too early to call it a day. And you're outside of an institution where the nurses wear belly shirts and smoke cigarettes and it should all feel significant, but doesn't.)

(MAGGIE and JACOB outside of Amy's care facility, unloading bags.)

JACOB. Let me help you carry it in.

KATHY. Not visiting hours –

Amy, let's wash up so I can clock out.

NANC-AY!!

NANCY! NANC-AY!! Where the hell is Nancy –

MAGGIE. Wait –

KATHY. You three need a minute?

JACOB. Yes, / yes –

MAGGIE. Please –

JACOB. – we need lots of minutes...

KATHY. Well, ya got like two.

(KATHY drags the bags inside.)

MAGGIE. Come here...

Amy – can I ask, before you go, how – how did you start working at the movie theater?

AMY. Is my job, Maggie.

MAGGIE. No, how'd you get there?

AMY. Work van.

MAGGIE. I'm wondering if you *chose* to work there, maybe you remember all our Sundays together growing up?

AMY. Well.

Sunday is my day off.

So.

JACOB. ...

MAGGIE. ...

JACOB. You – you do like the movies?

AMY. Jake, sometimes movies are good. Sometimes bad.
But you pay the same. No fair.

JACOB. This is – very true.

AMY. ...

MAGGIE. ...

JACOB. ...

AMY. You, me?

MAGGIE. You, me, and Jake.

AMY. Jake's my brother though.

MAGGIE. Yes –

AMY. You, me, Jake, at the movies, *no Kathy* –

MAGGIE. *Yes.*

Yes! – you remember?

JACOB. And Dad too. Dad too, and Mom.

Dad would drive us there.

AMY. But Dad die.

Mom die, they cannot see movies.

JACOB. But before –

MAGGIE. When we were kids?

JACOB. Do you remember –

MAGGIE. All of us together –?

> *(Beat.)*

AMY. Nick Nolte ask me to be his girlfriend at the movies.
He say *I like you* at the movies.
He say *You make my eyes look at you.*
So I say *Leave me alone, I be your girlfriend.*
Now he call me on the phone.

He say, "You tired? You eating dinner?"

I say, "You tired? You eating dinner?"

It's nice when somebody asks about your day at nighttime.

So I kiss him on the cheeks.

And he – he-he-he-he loves me.

JACOB. We love you too –

MAGGIE. Do you know that?

AMY. ...

...

You my friend?

MAGGIE. *Family.* Family, Amy, is all we have.

AMY. Jake's my brother.

JACOB. Yes, exactly.

AMY. Brother not family.

Sister not family.

Mom, dad, brother, sister means *friend.*

You are my friend.

I have lots of friends.

You my friend?

MAGGIE. ...?

JACOB. ...?

> (**KATHY** *appears and* **AMY** *sees her.*)

KATHY. – all set?! Come on, they're not gonna pay more overtime.

AMY. – see you next time. See you, bye!

> (**AMY** *nonchalantly waves and exits.* **KATHY** *doesn't acknowledge them further and drags Amy's bags into the home.*)

MAGGIE. ...

JACOB. ...

MAGGIE. ...

JACOB. ...

MAGGIE. ...

JACOB. – do you remember dropping Amy off, at the end of our visits?

MAGGIE. Yeah... Someone would always come out and get her, take her inside.

...Why didn't we ever try to go in?

JACOB. We were sitting in the back seat.

Of a warm car.

Half-asleep.

MAGGIE. Mom and Dad up front –

JACOB. Always arguing.

MAGGIE. – laughing too.

JACOB. Being driven home by two people who –
Seemed to know where they were going.

       (MAGGIE and JACOB get into the car.)

       (Into the front seats for the first time.)

       (JACOB slams on the horn and yells.)

       (MAGGIE yells too.)

       (They stop.)

       (They sit.)

MAGGIE. *Where do we go now?*

13.

(*A movie theater preparing for its feature presentation. Trumpets. Pop-corn advertising. The movie is about to begin.*)

(**BOBBY** *and* **AMY** *sit in movie theater seats, in an isolated pool of light.*)

BOBBY. Go pick our seats.

I like your new place – seems nice. You happy there?

AMY. ...

BOBBY. – what's your uh, what're your new roommates' names –

Heard they moved you to a new room.

AMY. ...

BOBBY. – you're taller than last time. Oh yeah, gettin' tall.

(**BOBBY** *extends his hand for a high five.*)

(*As* **AMY** *goes for it,* **BOBBY** *pulls his hand back and slicks it into his hair.*)

Down low.

Too slow.

AMY. – hey –!

BOBBY. – while your mom, sister, and brother park the car, I'll get ya set up here.

I got ya licorice this time.

AMY. – what color.

BOBBY. I *remember* what color.

Red.

And these.

– just came out, called Skittles.

I can't stop eatin' 'em, don't tell your mom.

...

I put 'em in a little bag, 'cause I been savin' all the reds for you.

...

All set.

Here, gimme that.

> (**BOBBY** *takes* **AMY**'s *straw and makes a worm grow in her hand with the straw wrapper.*)

...

...

...

AMY. *Magic.*

BOBBY. We gotta be quiet now, okay?

AMY. They good guys or bad?

BOBBY. Hard to tell sometimes.

But I barely pay attention.

On the way home your mom asks me about the movie.

I dunno what to –

...

'Cause I'm only ever watchin' *you.*

> (**AMY** *steps away from him.*)

Hey –

Get in your seat. – your movie's about to start –

> (*And away from him.*)

– when your brother comes and asks for your candy, what do ya say –

AMY. *Forget it, Jake. It's Chinatown.*

> (*Everything falls away but the movie's flicker. A giant, bright, and beautifully red movie theater curtain drops, closing off everything onstage but* **AMY**. *She steps forward, alone and dead center, as the preview sounds swell.*)

---

*A license to produce *Amy and the Orphans* does not include a performance license for any third-party or copyrighted music. Licensees should create an original composition or use music in the public domain. For further information, please see Music Use Note on page 3.

14.

AMY. I have always depended on the kindness of strangers.
But no more.
I'm mad as hell and I'm not gonna take it anymore!!
I am *serious*.
Don't call me Shirley.
I'm Bond.
James Bond.
I'm Thelma AND Louise.
You talkin' to me??
We're not in Kansas anymore.
You talkin' to me??
You're gonna need a bigger boat.
You talkin' to *me*???
Frankly my dear I don't give a damn.
I'm ready for my close-up Mr. DeMille.
You ain't heard nothin' yet!
Who the fuck do you think you're talking to?
You can't handle the truth.
Nobody puts baby in the corner.
I'll have what she's having 'cause I'm king of the world!
I'm walkin' here, I'm walkin' here!
I'm a human being, goddamnit.
MY LIFE HAS VALUE.
You don't understand.
I coulda been a contender.
I coulda been somebody.
I coulda been somebody.
I coulda been somebody.
I coulda been somebody.
...
...

Go ahead.

Make.
My.
Day.